Watch Those Trash Cans!

Written by Jo Windsor
Illustrated by Brent Chambers

Rigby

Big Bird said to Little Bird,
"Come here, Little Bird!
Watch me!
I'll show you how to fly.
This is what you do."

The big bird went up and down and around and . . . **oops!**

Big Bird said to Little Bird,
"Come here, Little Bird!
Watch me!
I'll show you how
to catch a little fish.
This is what you do."

The big bird went up
and up and down
and . . . **oops!**

5

Big Bird said to Little Bird,
"Come here, Little Bird!
Watch me!
I'll show you how
to land in a tree.
Watch me and you will see."

Big Bird went up and over.
He put his legs out
and . . . **oops!**

Big Bird said to Little Bird,
"Come here, Little Bird!
Watch me.
I'll show you how
to get some food.
This is what you do."

Big Bird flew up
and down and around
and . . . **oops!**
He landed on the trash can.
The lid opened
and Big Bird fell in.

The dump truck came
to get the trash.
It flipped the can and
out flew Big Bird.

Little Bird looked at Big Bird.
"You showed me how to fly.
You showed me how to fish.
You showed me how to land.
And you showed me how
to watch out for trash cans!"

A Rebus

Big Bird showed how to fly. He showed how to catch a . He showed how to land in a . He showed how to look out for . And showed how to watch out for !

Guide Notes

Title: Watch Out for Trash Cans!
Stage: Early (3) – Blue

Genre: Fiction
Approach: Guided Reading
Processes: Thinking Critically, Exploring Language, Processing Information
Written and Visual Focus: Rebus Writing

THINKING CRITICALLY
(sample questions)
* What do you think this story could be about?
* What do you know about how birds learn to fly?
* Look at pages 2 and 3. Why do you think Big Bird flew into the window?
* Look at pages 6 and 7. What do you think the cat would like to do to Big Bird?
* Where else do you think Big Bird could have gotten food from?
* What do you think Big Bird should do next time he is teaching Little Bird?

EXPLORING LANGUAGE

Terminology
Title, cover, illustrations, author, illustrator

Vocabulary
Interest words: dump, flipped
High-frequency words (new): watch, show, around, opened, window
Positional words: up, down, around, over

Print Conventions
Capital letter for sentence beginnings and names (**B**ig **B**ird, **L**ittle **B**ird), periods, exclamation marks, quotation marks, commas, ellipses